THE SUSPICIOUS CASE OF A DOG SPA CRIME

CURLY BAY ANIMAL RESCUE COZY MYSTERY BOOK 15

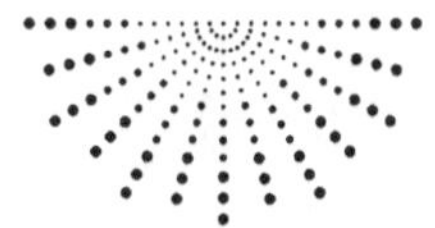

DONNA DOYLE

PUREREAD.COM

CONTENTS

CHAPTER ONE

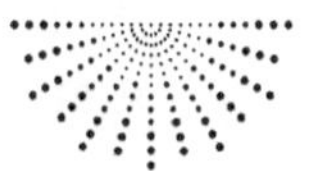

"No tags, no microchip, and no owners have come forward to claim him," Officer Jacobs explained as he handed the little dog over the counter. "He seems sweet enough, especially given the condition he's in. I imagine he's been out on his own for quite some time."

"Oh, you poor baby!" Courtney reached out for the dog, who instantly snuggled against her chest as soon as he was in her arms. His dark fur was matted and filthy, and his nails were grown out long enough that it had to be uncomfortable for him to walk. He gazed up at her with hope in his liquid black eyes.

"I know. He's a real heartbreaker." Officer Jacobs shook his head. "I'm glad you had the space for him.

We've only got so much room at the pound, and I just keep finding more and more of them on the streets."

"Such a shame." Courtney gently stroked the little dog's head. She was glad that she had such a good relationship with the animal control officer, who would call her up every time they got a dog whose owners couldn't be found. Even the shelter had limited room, but the foster program Courtney had established did make a difference. "Have you given him a name?"

Officer Jacobs grinned. "Bruce. I know it's a little ironic, since he's so shy and sweet, but I thought maybe it would give him some hope for the future."

"Bruce works for me."

The little dog gave a timid shake of his tail.

"I think it works for him, too! Thanks again. I'll keep you updated and let you know when he finds his forever home."

"I'd appreciate that." Officer Jacobs reached across the counter to give Bruce one last scratch behind the ears before he left to resume his duties.

"Come on, baby. I've got someone you need to meet." Courtney carried the little dog over to the spa and hotel side of the building. Dora was dreamily listening to classical music as she carefully clipped the rather impressive coat of a prize-winning cocker spaniel. The dog stood with his chin held high as his groomer stepped back to inspect her own work and ensure that not a single hair was out of place.

Dora was in her groove, doing what she did best, but she put her scissors down as soon as her eyes flicked up and spotted Bruce. She turned off the radio. "What do we have here? And I mean that literally. The poor thing doesn't even quite look like a dog!"

"I know. Officer Jacobs just dropped him off. His name is Bruce. I think under all this fur he's probably a Scottish terrier or maybe a mix. What do you think?"

To keep her client safe, Dora unclipped the cocker spaniel from the grooming table and put him back in his kennel before she came and took Bruce from Courtney. "That seems reasonable. I guess we'll find out for sure once he gets his hair cut. And a bath! You don't smell very nice, little boy!" She said the last part in a soft, singsong voice so that Bruce wouldn't think he was in trouble for something that wasn't his fault.

Courtney had to smile. All of those who worked at the Curly Bay Pet Hotel and Rescue understood that tone of voice was incredibly important when it came to animals, especially those who'd been abused or abandoned. Bruce obviously approved since he gave Dora a little wag of his tail as he began sniffing her shirt.

"Let me get a quick picture of him," Courtney said as she pulled her cell phone from the back pocket of her jeans. She hated to have to document such neglect, but she knew it would serve as a great contrast once Bruce was groomed. Photos like that not only would help Bruce get a new home, but once she had them posted on social media and their website it would serve as yet another point to the community on how important it was to take care of their pets.

Dora set Bruce carefully down on a grooming table and held him still with comforting hands while he had his picture taken. "He'll look like a completely different dog by the time I'm done with him. I'll give him that new terrier cut my spa clients have been asking for. There's no reason he can't look his best, no matter what side of the building he's on. Isn't that right, Bruce? Who's a good boy? I think you are!"

Bruce put his ears flat and pranced a little on the table.

"Mr. Personality here will have a home in no time," Courtney predicted. "If you've got him, I'll head back into the office and get him put in the system."

"Yep, you're all mine, Brucey boy! Let's trim off some of these knots and get you in the tub. You're stinking up the place. Yes, you are! Who's a stinky sweety?" Dora's enthusiastic babytalk followed Courtney out of the grooming area.

She was surprised to see Ms. O'Donnell waiting for her with a stranger in tow. Though Ms. O'Donnell was the owner of the place, she rarely actually came in. Instead, she left it up to Courtney to decide how things should be run.

"Courtney, there you are! I'd like you to meet my friend, Linda Nicholson. Linda is going to be volunteering at the shelter full time for the next couple of weeks." Mrs. O'Donnell lifted her chin proudly.

"It's nice to meet you," Linda said softly. She was probably in her forties, with light blond hair that curled just a little bit as it came down around her shoulders. Her eyes were big, soft, and maybe a little uncertain.

In a lot of ways, she reminded Courtney of the rescue animals they took in. She held out her hand. "It's nice to meet you, too. It's not very often that we get people in who can commit to volunteering full time, and goodness knows we can use the help. There's always something going on around here. Do you have any experience?"

"I love animals, and I've always had a pet or two. That's about the extent of it, I'm afraid." Linda bit her lip uncertainly as she glanced at Ms. O'Donnell.

"That's all the experience you need!" her friend assured her. "Courtney here will get you filled in on everything you need to do, and none of it is all that difficult. Having a compassionate heart is the biggest requirement, and I know you've got that."

Courtney could tell that Linda was extremely nervous. She knew there was no reason to be, but people—just like animals—often got anxious in new situations. "Peppa," she said softly to the big beagle mix snoring under her desk. "Hey, sweetie. Come on out here and meet Linda."

Opening first one eye and then the other, Peppa made a rather dramatic show of stretching before she left her bed and came out wagging her tail. She wagged it a little harder when she saw Linda.

"This is Peppa," Courtney said, making the introductions. "She came in as a stray a couple of years ago. She was terrified of everyone and everything, and she couldn't even walk on a leash. I fostered her at home, and I ended up adopting her. Now she comes in with me every day, and she's essentially part of the team."

"Hi, Peppa." Linda crouched down and held out her hand.

The dog gave it an obligatory sniff before shoving her head underneath Linda's fingers and demanding pets.

Linda laughed. "You're a lovely thing, aren't you?" Linda's uncertainty melted into laughter and smiles as she scratched Peppa's chin and rubbed her shoulders.

Courtney smiled to herself. She'd learned a lot about dogs and cats since she moved away from the city and began her job here, and she thought maybe she was starting to learn a lot about people, too.

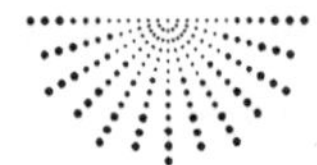

CHAPTER TWO

"I'll leave you ladies to it," Ms. O'Donnell said with a smile as she grabbed her purse. "I'm off to talk to the travel agent about my next cruise. I'll be back later this afternoon."

When she was gone, Courtney turned to her new volunteer. "I'll show you around. Have you ever been here before?"

Linda shook her head. "I can't say that I have. I've kept meaning to, what with how much Melanie is always going on about it, but I've just been too busy up until now." She paused, clasping her hands in front of her and looking down at the floor. Her eyes shimmered with tears when she finally looked back up at Courtney. "You see, my husband passed away a few weeks ago. We were planning to retire early and do some traveling, but we're not going to get that chance now. I need something to keep myself distracted."

"Oh, Linda. I'm so sorry to hear that." Courtney had never been married before. She'd been engaged once, to a greedy corporate ladder-climber who'd had her sacked as soon as he felt she'd served her purpose. Courtney had forgiven Sam and moved on since then. Even so, she couldn't possibly imagine the grief this woman must be going through.

Linda flapped a dismissive hand in the air and shook her head. "No, that's all right. We don't need to dwell on that. That's not why I'm here."

"Right." If Linda needed a distraction, then the shelter was sure to provide one. "We'll start at one end of the building and work our way through. Did Ms. O'Donnell have you fill out any of the volunteer paperwork?"

"No, she didn't."

That figured. Ms. O'Donnell had a wonderful heart. It was her interest in financing the shelter that'd inspired her to start up the hotel and spa. But she wasn't great when it came to running a business, and that was exactly why Courtney had a job. "No problem. Let's head this way. The shelter is over here." She headed toward the west side of the building. "We keep the cats and dogs in separate rooms. I think you'll see why in a minute."

"Oh!" Linda clapped her hands over her ears as they entered the dog kennel. "Do they always bark this much?"

"Off and on, yes," Courtney shouted over the din. She was used to it by now. "Anytime something changes, which could be a person or a dog coming in or out. They have a good amount of space, but this still isn't the same as a real home for them."

"Poor things."

Courtney showed her the clipboard on each dog's cage that showed the last time they were fed and walked. She gave an overview of where all the supplies were and how often the cages should be cleaned. Just down the hall, they were met with the relative silence of the cat room.

"This is much better," Linda said, visibly relaxing her shoulders as they walked in. "I do like dogs, and I understand why they bark so much, but it really echoes in there!"

A tuxedo cat in a nearby cage gave her a pitiful meow.

"Yes, I hear you, too," Linda said sympathetically.

In here, Courtney explained the daily procedures with the cats. "Just like the dogs, they have their names on their cages. We try to take only one out at a time, so they don't escape, and we keep a spare cage open so that you're not always trying to clean around them. Most of them will take all the cuddling they can get."

"Dear little things." Linda poked her finger between the bars of a cage holding an orange tabby. It purred and rubbed its cheek against her.

Soon enough, they headed over to the grooming area. Dora was working away on Bruce, with mountains of dark hair falling all over the table and the floor while she manned the clippers. "Dora, this is Linda. She's a friend of Ms. O'Donnell's, and she's going to be volunteering full time for a little while."

Dora turned off the clippers. "I'd shake your hand, but I'm all covered in dog fur. Of course, you will be soon enough!" she laughed.

"You seem to be in a good mood," Courtney noted. Most of the time, Dora was a quiet woman and even a bit surly.

"I can't help it. Just look at this little guy." She nodded toward her client on the grooming table, who'd rolled over onto his back and was begging for belly rubs. "He's difficult, because he won't stand up and be still for me, but he's being so darn sweet about it I can't even get mad."

Linda blinked at all the hair that'd come off the little dog. "That's quite a change!"

"He needed it." Courtney gave her a rundown of Bruce's circumstances before he arrived at the shelter. "We'll help him out and give him a new home. Dora, what kind of things could Linda help you out with in here once I get her paperwork squared away?"

"There's plenty! Sweeping, cleaning out the tub, and I can always use an extra hand with a brush."

Courtney beamed. She knew Dora could be a bit protective of her job and her area, so it was nice to see that she was just as excited about having a volunteer as Courtney was. She had no doubt that Dora would keep the scissors to herself, but Linda wouldn't run out of things to do. "Wonderful. Let's head back to the office."

"Is there anything you'll need me to do in here?" Linda asked as she settled into a chair in front of Courtney's desk.

"I hadn't thought about that," Courtney admitted as she handed over a volunteer application and a pen. So far, most of their volunteers just came in for a Saturday morning or helped when they had an adoption event. "I suppose there's always some filing or organizing to be done. I think you're going to be a great addition here!"

Linda paused in filling out the application to pet Peppa, who'd come over and rested her head on Linda's lap. "It's going to be wonderful."

A few minutes later, Courtney exchanged the application for a waiver and a few other forms that Linda needed to sign. She knew there was no need for the application to go through any sort of approval process, since Ms. O'Donnell had recommended her directly, but she still needed to get all the information into the system. She paused as she typed it all in. "Your middle name is Wheeler? How interesting."

"It was my maiden name, actually," Linda explained. "I decided to keep it as part of my name when I got married, since it was already on so much of my other documents."

"That makes sense." She quickly input the rest of the information, which didn't take long, and started up a new file with Linda's name on it. "That should just about do it. I think Jessi's back from lunch, so I'll introduce you to her and she can let you know what she needs."

Linda stood up, and she cast a grateful look at Courtney. "I just want you to know how much I appreciate this."

"Me? You're the one who's volunteering all your time and energy," Courtney replied with a little laugh. She tucked a strand of her dark hair behind her ear as she bent down to lock the file folder away in her drawer.

"Yes, but it really does mean a lot to me. Kevin's passing was very unexpected. I was terribly busy at first, dealing with all the arrangements and just being sad. Once the funeral was over, my life felt so completely empty. I'd distanced myself from my family a long time ago because there was always so much trouble and drama with them, and I knew I needed to keep my own mental health a priority. I know that was the right thing to do, but I had to wonder once I found myself completely alone. I know having some time to help the animals here will be wonderful for me, so I really am grateful."

"They'll be very grateful for you, too," Courtney replied. She'd seen the sweet and appreciative looks from dogs and cats so many times. "Can I ask you something?"

"Sure."

"Ms. O'Donnell said you'd be volunteering here for a few weeks. What are your plans after that?" Before Courtney had known that Linda's husband passed away, her guess had been that Linda just had some extra vacation time to burn. It turned out her free time was a much bigger problem.

Linda lifted a shoulder. "I think I'll find myself a part-time job, something that will give me a little income and something to do without putting my nose all the way to the grindstone. I've started looking, but I haven't found anything just yet."

"Well, we're happy to keep you occupied until you do. Let's go find Jessi and get you started."

Later that afternoon, Ms. O'Donnell came back from the travel agent and cornered Courtney in the office. "Well? How's she doing?"

Courtney made a face. She knew Ms. O'Donnell was the woman who signed her paychecks, but that didn't mean she wasn't going to be honest with her. She glanced over her shoulder to make sure nobody else was in the office. "Not all that great."

"Really? But she loves animals, and she was so excited at the chance!" Her boss furrowed her brow.

"Oh, there's no doubt that she's good with animals. Every one she touches seems happy to be near her, and it's obvious that Linda really cares about them. But it's like she instantly forgets everything she's asked to do, and she gets mixed up. Jessi asked her specifically to take Peter out for a walk, but she took Willow instead. I told her to give certain cats wet food, but she gave them dry. I'm not sure what to think." She hated to have to give this report, but Linda was becoming more of a problem than a help.

Ms. O'Donnell frowned. "Maybe for now just keep her on simpler tasks. Linda's a good person, and I don't think she'd be having such a hard time if she wasn't grieving. Kevin meant the absolute world to her."

"Yeah, from what she told me, it sounds like he was all she had," Courtney agreed. "Don't get me wrong. I'm glad she's here and that she wants to help. I'm just worried that it's going to cause problems in the smooth way we like to run things."

"Don't worry about that," Ms. O'Donnell replied. "It's only her first day, and everything will get better."

CHAPTER THREE

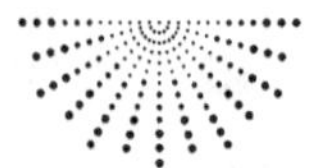

Unfortunately, things didn't really get better. "It's really frustrating," she said to her friend Lisa on her way home from work a few days later. "I don't want to complain about anybody who's working for free, but it's just not working out at all. I thought I would be pretty safe in asking her to mop the floors, but she used the wrong cleaner and now they're sticky."

"That does sound like a problem, especially in combination with all the dog and cat hair," Lisa sympathized. Lisa had spent a little bit of time volunteering at the shelter when she wasn't busy working at the library, and she'd adopted a dog and a cat. "What are you going to do?"

"There's not much I can do besides wait it out." Courtney flicked on her turn signal and waited for traffic before she pulled into the grocery store parking lot. "She's not going to stay forever, and she's friends with the boss, so I'm stuck."

"I'm sorry. Call me later this week and we'll go out for lunch. In the meantime, I think my meatloaf is burning. Talk to you later!"

Courtney hung up and glared at the bright pink neon lights in the little store next to the grocers. It was one of those new video gaming parlors, the sort of place where people could go in and play slots without going all the way to Vegas. It hadn't really registered on Courtney's radar before, since she didn't gamble, but she was irritated enough now that just the brightly lit sign was annoying. "You stay here," she said to Peppa as she opened the door. "I'm just going to get a couple of things for our dinner, and I'll be right back."

Used to going literally everywhere with Courtney, Peppa wagged her tail and sat quietly.

She got out just as a man walked out of Rose's Gaming. He had one hand shoved in his pocket and a jacket tucked in the crook of his elbow. In the other hand he was holding his cell phone, and he hardly even looked up as he started down the sidewalk.

Courtney shook her head. Doing that was going to get him run over, but it wasn't as though she could stop him. Her mind easily drifted right back to Linda when she heard a shout. Courtney paused just a few feet from the grocery store entrance. It's yellow fluorescent lighting invited her to come on in and get the buns she needed for sloppy Joes, but there was something in that shout that intrigued her. She heard it again and looked off to her right, where the man who'd come out of the gaming parlor stood near the corner of the building.

"Just stop, okay! I'll fix it!" he shouted.

"No, you won't! You never have, and you never will!" It was a woman's voice that called out just before a shot rang against the buildings and echoed through the downtown area.

Courtney instantly crouched to the ground, watching with wide eyes as the man staggered and fell to the sidewalk, clutching his chest. That allowed Courtney to see the woman who was standing right in front of him, the woman who'd just shot him at point-blank range.

It was Linda.

Her eyes were glazed over in terror. She still held the gun out at arm's length, a thin stream of smoke drifting up into the night air from the end of the barrel. Her hand started shaking after a moment, and then she dropped the gun to her side before turning around and charging down the alley.

Courtney felt the warm grit of the concrete entryway under her fingers, and it reminded her that this wasn't just a dream. Her legs were stiff with fear as she forced herself to stand up. Adrenaline flooded through her system as her heart hammered in her chest. The blood was coursing through her so fast that she thought she might pass out as she propelled herself across the parking lot.

Someone came out of Rose's Gaming just as she reached the man sprawled on the sidewalk. "What happened?"

"He's been shot. Call the police!" Courtney didn't even turn to look up at whoever she'd just spoken to. Her focus was entirely on the victim. "It's all right," she said as she heard sirens start up in the distance. Someone must have already called when they heard the shot. "Help is on the way. You'll be all right."

The man shook his head, barely conscious.

Courtney spotted the jacket he'd had tucked through his elbow just a moment ago and snatched it up, seeing it as the quickest access to some sort of compress. She folded it into the thickest pad she could before she pressed it to his chest. There was no telling whether she was doing any real good, but she had to at least try.

The man from the gaming parlor reemerged. "The police and an ambulance are on their way. Is there anything I can do?"

Courtney shrugged helplessly. "I don't know a lot of first aid, and especially for gunshot wounds. You?"

"Not much beyond what I've learned on TV." He knelt on the other side of the victim. His brown hair was swept back to show off a rather prominent nose and dark eyes. He touched the man's hand. "It's cold. I think he's going into shock."

"The ambulance is here," Courtney said with great sigh of relief as the big white vehicle swerved into the parking lot and two uniformed paramedics jumped out.

"Step back! We'll handle this."

Courtney gladly got out of the way while they did their job. The paramedics worked quickly as they loaded the man into the ambulance, but Courtney knew he'd be dead before they ever reached the hospital.

Feeling dizzy and reeling from everything she'd just seen, Courtney sat down on a parking curb and braced her elbows on her knees. She glanced back at her vehicle, seeing that Peppa was alert and watching the activity from the car, but she seemed all right. Courtney hated to leave her in there, but the weather was nice, and it was probably a much safer place for the pup for the moment.

The police had arrived now, and there were so many spinning lights bouncing off the clustered downtown buildings that it was making Courtney's head spin as well. She closed her eyes against it until she felt a hand on her shoulder.

"Hey. You okay?"

It was the guy from the gaming parlor. "I'm all right. Just dizzy."

"I'll get you a drink." He disappeared inside and came back out with two bottles of cold water and sat down next to her. "Crazy stuff, huh?"

"Definitely. I was just supposed to grab a couple things from the store." She pressed the icy bottle against her forehead. It felt good, but it didn't quite abate the nausea that was rolling in her stomach. Courtney had seen some other crazy stuff in the time she lived in Curly Bay, but this hadn't been easy.

A uniformed officer that Courtney didn't recognize came over as the ambulance sped away. "I'll need to get statements from each of you. Separately, if you don't mind."

The man stood up. "I think she needs a minute. I'll go first." He followed the officer back toward the squad car.

It was her turn before she knew it. Courtney got up, surprised that she was feeling much steadier now. She leaned against the squad car, tempted to ask if they could just call in Detective Fletcher instead. She was used to talking to him, and she'd feel a lot more comfortable. But even if the police were willing to do so, Courtney didn't want to wait around. She just wanted this to be over with.

"Can you tell me what happened here, ma'am?" The officer's mouth was a grim line as he waited for her answer.

She did the best she could. Courtney could remember it all vividly, and yet no words that came out of her mouth seemed quite sufficient for describing the scene. It didn't take long, at least, because it'd all happened within the span of a few minutes.

"And can you tell me any information about the victim?" The officer fired off his next question as soon as she was done. "No. I didn't know him. I'd never seen him."

"Did you see the gunman."

"It was a woman." Courtney closed her eyes. She could so easily see her, even in the dark shadows that crept out of the alley and tried to battle with the brilliant sign. The pink of the neon had flashed across her cheeks and in her eyes. The lighting was so weird, but there was no doubt in Courtney's mind of exactly what she'd seen. It was all right there in her mind, even if it didn't make sense. "It was Linda Nicholson."

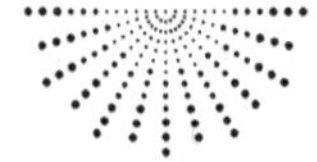

CHAPTER FOUR

"You're kidding," Jessi gasped.

"I'm afraid not." Courtney stared down at her cup of coffee. It'd long gone cold as she'd told her tale. There wasn't much point in trying to keep it under wraps. The man's murder had been all over the evening news, and then again in the morning. The victim's name hadn't yet been released, and Courtney knew she'd be watching for that update over the next couple of days. "It was pretty crazy."

Dora shook her head. "I can't believe that Curly Bay has turned into the sort of place where you can get shot right in the middle of downtown when it's hardly even dark outside. It used to be that people didn't even bother locking their doors or windows around here."

"Maybe they didn't, but that doesn't mean they shouldn't have," Jessi replied. "And who knows? There could've been some vendetta, or a deal gone wrong. It probably wasn't random."

"If it has to happen, then at least they could keep it off the street and out of sight of the general public," Dora remarked with a sneer. "I know I personally don't want to have to see that."

"Trust me. You don't," Courtney agreed. She took a sip of her coffee, thought about swapping it out for a hot mug, and then decided she didn't have the energy to bother.

Realizing the coldness of her words, Dora patted Courtney on the shoulder. "I'm sorry. It's just a little shocking."

Courtney drew in a deep breath. A jolt of nerves twisted through her stomach as she blew it out, debating. She'd told them all about hearing the gunshot and waiting for the ambulance, but Jessi and Dora didn't know the most shocking part just yet. Courtney almost didn't want to tell them. It didn't seem fair, but it also didn't seem fair to keep it a secret. "The worst part is that I know who the killer was. It was Linda."

The silence that fell over the three of them was so quiet that it buzzed in Courtney's ears. She saw the disbelief and surprise that she felt in her own heart reflected in their eyes. "I know. It's hard to believe."

Dora swallowed. "I guess that explains why she hasn't been here yet this morning."

Jessi leaned forward. "Did you tell the police?"

"Well, of course she did!" Dora retorted. She paused and looked at Courtney. "Didn't you?"

"Yes," she said with a little bit of a laugh despite how completely drained her body and mind felt. "I saw the whole thing, and I couldn't exactly keep information like that to myself. I felt kind of bad about it. I like Linda on a personal level."

"You did what you had to do. Nobody would expect you to put yourself at risk by hiding something like that." Dora patted Courtney on the arm.

Jessi shrugged. "I can't say this is how I wanted it to happen, but it kind of works out for us."

Courtney looked at her employee, confused. "What do you mean?"

"Look, I wouldn't want anyone to get killed or even injured, but if Linda goes to jail then she won't be volunteering here. I know, that's horrible cold and callous, but I'm not sad to be rid of her. No matter how much her heart might be in the right place when it comes to cats and dogs, she can't keep a single thing straight. Even after just a few days, I was starting to wonder how long I could stand going around behind her and fixing her mistakes." Jessi swiped her hands over her face and down the sides of her neck, making her dangling earrings, which were composed of numerous little bits of shell, jingle.

"That's true enough," Dora agreed. "I asked her to clean out the wash tub in the grooming area, and she somehow managed to clog the drain. And she missed all the fur under the tables when I had her sweep."

Courtney frowned down into her cup. "I know she was going through a hard time. Her husband had passed away. I just don't understand why she would turn around and kill someone else. Maybe I never will."

"Are you all right?" Dora asked gently. "We'd all understand if you want a day or two off work."

"No. I mean, yes, I'm fine. But no, I don't want any time off. I'd much rather be here and doing something useful than just moping around my house and trying to figure out what to do with myself. I appreciate it, though." She paused as the bell over the front door rang. "And it sounds like I have something to do right now. Excuse me." Courtney got up and headed into the front lobby, grateful for whoever had just walked in the door but fully aware of the looks her employees were exchanging behind her. She couldn't blame them for being worried. It wasn't every day you witnessed a murder, and especially when it was committed by someone you know. Courtney sighed. She'd just have to deal with it.

Mrs. McKenzie was standing impatiently in the lobby, tapping the toe of her pale pink flat against the linoleum as though she'd been waiting there for hours instead of a few seconds. She was one of the wealthy elite in Curly Bay, the kind who went to the country club and knew all the inside gossip about all the richest people in the county. Mrs. McKenzie was a little bit younger than most of the crowd that ran around with Mrs. Throgmorton, one of the best patrons of the shelter. Today she wore a pale pink pencil skirt that perfectly matched her shoes and a cream top. A thick gold chain hung around her neck, a simple but obvious statement.

"Courtney, there you are!" Mrs. McKenzie was always a little too loud, but Courtney had heard she'd only recently come into her wealth, through marriage. Maybe she was just worried nobody would notice her. "Angus is here for a few days while I have some flooring put down. He won't want to have to deal with the workmen, so I guess I'm stuck doing that on my own! He needs a bath and a haircut desperately. I have some people coming over this weekend, and I need my little man to look absolutely perfect!"

"I'm sure Dora can achieve that for you." Courtney quickly checked the client in on the computer before she reached over the counter for Angus. The dark terrier mix allowed himself to be handed over, but he showed no interest in the person who was holding him now, nor did he seem to care that his owner was now on the other side of the table. That was how he'd been ever since Courtney had first met him. He was the most aloof little dog she'd ever met.

"Do you think you could have her give him that haircut she's been doing lately? I don't know what she calls it, but I saw it on Mrs. Garza's little Yorkie. Sort of shorter than the cut Angus usually gets?" She tapped her manicured fingers, glazed in that same pale pink, on the counter for emphasis.

"I know just the one you mean. I'll make a note and get that arranged for you. Anything else? A massage or a paw mask?" When Courtney had first come to work here, she'd thought a lot of the extra services they offered were a little ridiculous. After all, what dog really needed nail polish or a special cologne? It turned out the answer was all the dogs who wore diamond collars and were spoiled silly by their rich owners. The good thing was that the animals seemed to like the extra treatments, and it created more funding for the shelter.

Mrs. McKenzie beamed at the idea. "Those would be lovely! His little tootsies are a bit rough, and maybe the massage will calm him down some. He's always so stern. Aren't you, my little baby?" She made kissy faces at her dog, who took absolutely no notice.

"Wonderful. I'll add that to the list." Courtney headed over into the grooming area and put Angus in a kennel. He gave her a dirty look over his shoulder as she closed the door. "I imagine that's exactly how Linda would look at me right now if she had the chance," Courtney muttered.

"What was that?" Dora asked as she walked into the room.

"Oh, nothing. I was just talking to Angus. You should know that your fancy haircut is really catching on. Mrs. McKenzie requested it for him."

Dora came up next to her as they both looked at the little dog. "Not that a cute little cut will do him much good. He always looks like such a crabby old man. I like him, though. He's always very well behaved on the table. I swear he knows exactly what I need him to do."

"I'm heading into the office to do some paperwork. I'll be putting in a supply order later this week, so let me know what you need." Courtney rubbed the back of her neck and headed for the door.

"Courtney."

She turned. "Yes?"

"I know you said you're fine, and I know you want to be here working, but don't be afraid to let us know if there's anything we can do to help. Really. We're worried about you, and even if you just need to take a long lunch break, we're happy to cover for you."

Courtney smiled. Dora could be just as aloof and distant as Angus, but deep down she was also incredibly nice. "Thank you. I'll keep that in mind."

As she sat back down at her desk and tried to get through the monthly reports that would be due next week, Courtney wondered if she just might have to take advantage of Dora's offer. The numbers on the page swam in front of her eyes as she once again saw Linda standing at the mouth of that dark alley. She couldn't concentrate on scheduling a few posts for the social media pages without wondering how a woman who seemed so sweet could just stand there and kill someone in cold blood. It didn't make the slightest bit of sense to her, and she was going to have to find a way for it not to drive her crazy.

CHAPTER FIVE

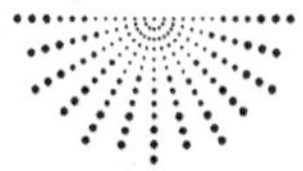

"Have you seen those soft dog treats?" Jessi asked as she walked through the office later that afternoon. "The ones I keep back for senior and sickly dogs?"

"I can't say that I have. I can order some, though." Courtney was finally starting to feel like she was getting some work done, but it'd been quite the fight. She'd poured what seemed like endless cups of coffee, only to have them all go cold on her desk by the time she finally remembered they were there. The only reason she'd been able to finish the midmorning snack she'd brought along was because she had to share it with Peppa, who was more than happy to take care of it for her. The monthly report was as complete as it could be until she had a few more figures finalized, and she'd moved on to paying the bills.

Jessi let out an exasperated sigh. "That would be great, except that I was hoping to use them right now. I swear, there's no telling where Linda put them. And I know she probably did put them somewhere, simply because I'd asked her not to use them unless I told her specifically. That's just how she operated."

Courtney pressed her lips together to stop herself from reminding Jessi not to get too mad at Linda, since the poor woman was grieving. Courtney had to remember, though, that the 'poor woman' was also a murderer. It'd been less than twenty-four hours, but she still wasn't sure she'd ever be able to wrap her head around that. "I'll put some on the list, and then I'll help you look for them. They've got to be around here somewhere."

"I hope so. I just took Pearl out for her walk, and I know she's expecting her treat. Ever since she had those teeth removed, I've been so worried about her." Jessi opened a cabinet that was supposed to only be for office supplies and poked around on the shelves.

"Poor old girl. I felt bad for her, but I know she's better off." Courtney got up from her desk. The treats were supposed to be in a high cabinet in the kennel, but she knew Jessi had already looked there. Randomly, she opened the doors under the little sink in the break area. "Found them."

"Thank goodness!" Jessi grabbed them and headed off toward the kennels. "I'm coming, Pearl!"

Courtney smiled. It was a strange feeling, but a nice one. It didn't last long, because Detective Fletcher was walking into the office as she returned to her desk.

"You don't have to look quite so unhappy to see me," the detective joked as he took a chair.

"I'm sorry. I just—I figure I know why you're here, and it's something I've been trying not to think about," Courtney admitted.

"You? *Not* thinking about a case? Now that's something I'd have to see to believe." Fletcher leaned back in his chair and studied her with those watery blue eyes of his. "I'd have thought you'd be all over this, looking for clues and figuring things out. You know, the usual."

"There's not much motivation to look for clues when I already know exactly who did it," Courtney pointed out. "I saw her myself. It's different this time."

"Maybe."

"What do you mean, maybe?" Courtney didn't like to see Detective Fletcher being the slightest bit evasive. He was usually straightforward, sometimes to a fault. "We're talking about someone who's been working right here alongside me for the past few days. Don't play with me."

"The fact that Linda Nicholson has been working here is exactly why I'm sitting in front of your desk right now," Fletcher replied. Peppa put her head in his lap, expecting the pets that she knew would come. He obliged. "What are the odds that you would get a new volunteer and then witness her murdering someone just a few days later?"

"That's exactly what I've been wondering myself," Courtney conceded. "Well, that and a few other things. Linda struck me as an incredibly nice person when I met her. I didn't think she had a mean bone in her body. She wasn't a particularly good volunteer, and there were plenty of complaints about her, but none of that had anything to do with her attitude or how well she got along with people."

Detective Fletcher scratched his head. "I agree. She does seem very nice. I had the chance to have a rather long interview with her myself. I can tell you from my own experience that nice doesn't necessarily translate to good or innocent, but I think it does in this case."

"What? What are you talking about?" Courtney jolted upright in her chair, causing Peppa to turn around and look at her owner in concern. "I saw Linda myself. I saw the entire thing!"

"I know. Calm down, Courtney. I'll explain everything to you, but be patient. After you'd given your statement to the officers at the scene, Mrs. Nicholson was taken into custody without any resistance. She was very confused, but we didn't even have to handcuff her. I personally prefer it when our job can be a little easier like that."

"And?" Courtney pressed, not all that concerned with how polite Linda might have been as she was put into the back of a cruiser.

"She was at home in her pajamas, getting ready to settle in for the evening with a movie and a snack. I'm pointing that out simply because someone who's just killed a man would probably be packing their bags and getting ready to leave town, and they certainly wouldn't answer the door." Detective Fletcher looked at her pointedly.

Courtney blinked. "I don't think I quite believe what I think you're telling me."

He shrugged. "You might as well. The victim's name was Tyler Lancaster. Linda has no idea who he is. She says she's never laid eyes on him before."

"Obviously, that's not true!" Courtney exclaimed. She was losing control of herself, she knew, but she just couldn't help it. This was crazy.

"You'd think so, but then we asked her where she was at the time of the murder. She claimed she'd gone to the mall over in Ruby Cove once she got done at the shelter. There's security footage of her vehicle pulling into the parking lot, and we have multitudes of footage showing her walking around the mall and going in and out of several stores. We were even able to double-check that against security footage from some of the individual stores. Her alibi is rock-solid, Courtney." Detective Fletcher studied her, waiting for her reaction. He was an older man, and the years of police work had put quite a few lines and wrinkles on his face. It made for quite the picture, like something out of an old movie.

Courtney swallowed. "Maybe they had the wrong date on the security cameras?" she asked in a small voice.

He shook his head. "It's her, and it's from last night. She left the shelter and went to the gas station, where we were also able to find footage. Then she headed over to the mall. She said it's something she started doing in the evenings after her husband passed away, just because she couldn't stand to be sitting at home alone all the time. Mostly, she doesn't even buy anything. It's just something to do, but it was a good thing she did, or she'd be in jail right now."

"So, you let her go." It wasn't a question but a statement, a horrified statement.

Fletcher leaned forward and folded his hands together on the edge of the desk. "Courtney, is there any chance that you could be mistaken in what you saw? That maybe you were tired, or the lighting was weird? Or maybe you were angry with Linda? Because while I don't know who did kill Tyler Lancaster, I definitely know it wasn't her."

Her mouth was completely dry. Courtney had been rattled enough just by being a witness to the shooting, but this was worse. "No." She choked on the word on the way out, so she cleared her throat and tried again. "No. I know what I saw. I'm not crazy, and I don't make things up. You know that."

"I do know that, so it's troubling. I thought it was best if I came down here myself and let you know. I expect Linda will be showing back up for her volunteer work, and I need you to understand that I'm already looking into his." He tapped the stubby end of one finger on the desk.

"So, you just expect me to go about my life, working right alongside a murderer?" she hissed.

"That's the thing, Courtney. She's not a murderer. She's innocent, or at the very least she's innocent until someone can prove otherwise. But," he paused and held that finger in the air, "that's not an invitation for you to come looking into this."

"And why shouldn't I?" Courtney had stumbled her way through a few cases before, and she and Detective Fletcher had often even worked together.

"You're too close to this one, first of all," he said softly. "Second, Mr. Lancaster ran himself deeply in debt. He had a big gambling problem, and not just at

Rose's. Depending on who he owed, it could be dangerous for you to go sticking your nose where it doesn't belong. Trust me on this one, Courtney."

She wanted to. She really did. But how could she just shrug it off and go back to work like nothing had happened? It was impossible! Courtney could see the serious look on his face, though, and most of the time Fletcher didn't bother asking her to mind her own business. She knew he wouldn't do it now if it weren't for a good reason. "You'll keep me updated?"

"Of course, I will. In the meantime, maybe you should go home and get some rest. Seeing what you saw—no matter who did it—is bound to be stressful." He gave Peppa one last pat on the head and stood up.

"It was, but I'll be here," she replied. Her tongue felt as stiff and dry as cardboard in her mouth, and she wasn't entirely sure her lungs were functioning. This felt like a nightmare or an episode of *The Twilight Zone.* She was fairly certain this was the worst case she'd ever been involved in.

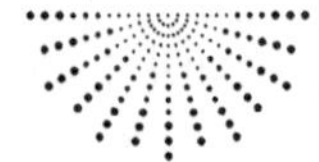

CHAPTER SIX

"Courtney?"

Courtney jolted in her desk chair. Her heart rattled around in her chest and adrenaline flooded her veins at the chipper voice behind her.

"Sorry. I didn't mean to startle you. I was just wondering where to find some more cat litter."

She didn't turn around because she didn't want Linda to see the look on her face. Courtney had been trying to hide her sheer terror of Linda ever since she'd come back to the office. Instead, she resumed writing the notes she was working on. "Should be in the supply room, near the back."

"I looked there already, and I didn't see it. Could you help me?"

Could she go into a supply closet at the back of the building, into a room where nobody would probably hear or pay any attention to a couple of random thumps or screams, with a killer? "Sure. No problem." What else was she supposed to do?

Did Linda know that Courtney was the one who was at the scene of the crime? Someone must have told her that a witness saw her, but did they give her name? Courtney wasn't sure of the legalities of that, but she hoped not. There was always a chance that Courtney had been backlit by the bright lights of the grocery store, and that even if Linda had looked directly at her she might not have recognized her.

"Thanks. I'm sorry," Linda said, wringing her hands together as they headed through the doorway and took a left. "I know Jessi already told me where it was. I think she's irritated with me, so I didn't want to ask her again."

"Why do you think she's irritated with you?" Courtney flicked on the switch and made sure to leave the door open behind her as she skirted around a pallet of dog food.

"Well, I just don't seem to be getting anything right. You know, this is exactly why employers only want to hire young folks, while their brains are still pliable. Jessi tells me to jump and while I'm trying to remember how to ask how high, I've already forgotten what I was supposed to do in the first place." She let out an embarrassed laugh.

"The cat litter is right here." Courtney found it exactly where it was supposed to be. The stack of heavy plastic buckets was hard to miss.

Linda pressed her fingertips to her forehead. "I'm so silly! I'm sorry to have pulled you away from whatever you were doing."

"It's all right." Courtney looked at her. Linda truly looked like someone you might run into in the produce section of the grocery store and strike up a random conversation about watermelons. She was sweet and gentle, and she seemed so genuine about wanting to do a good job even though she didn't get paid. If someone else had told Courtney they'd seen Linda commit a murder, then she wouldn't believe them either. "We've got it taken care of now, and I'm sure you'll get used to everything soon enough."

"Thank you," Linda said genuinely.

The two of them carried some litter into the cat room, and Courtney had to wonder how someone like Detective Fletcher could stand his work. It had to drive him crazy when someone was feigning innocence and he knew they were guilty. Either that, or he'd gotten so used to it over the years that it didn't bother him anymore. Courtney knew she definitely would never go into law enforcement for herself. She preferred to be able to sleep at night instead of having all the what if's floating through her mind.

She stepped out to the lobby just as Mrs. McKenzie came storming into the building. She'd swapped her pale pink outfit for one in jade green. Her pumps, her dress, and even the bangle bracelets on her wrist all matched perfectly. She carried Angus in her arms as usual, and even he had a jade green leash on. "Courtney, we need to talk!"

Courtney raised her brows. Angus had just been in the other day, and there shouldn't be anything he needed. That meant there had to be something wrong. "Sure. What can I do for you?" she asked calmly.

Mrs. McKenzie tossed her dark hair behind her shoulders and threw her chin in the air as she held Angus out slightly. "There's something wrong with

Angus! He hasn't been the same since I picked him up!"

Puzzled, Courtney held out her hands. "What seems to be the matter? Can I see him?"

"You can, but it's nothing you'll be able to see with the naked eye!" She handed the dog over and fisted her empty hands on her hips.

Angus snuggled down in Courtney's arms and shoved his face into the crook of her elbow. That was certainly unusual behavior for such a standoffish dog, but not unwelcome. "Well, hello to you, too," Courtney said.

"You see! It's that right there! Angus would never have done that before!" Mrs. McKenzie screeched.

The poor dog shook a little and buried himself further into Courtney's arms. "I don't see any harm in him being a little bit cuddly. Dogs and cats get needy and insecure sometimes, just like people do."

But her customer shook her head emphatically. "It's not just that he's 'a little cuddly.' He normally sleeps on his own little bed in the corner of my room, but last night he kept jumping right up into bed with me. He's completely forgotten our morning routine, and he wanted to eat *before* he went outside instead of after. And don't even get me started on what happened when I took him to the dog park!"

Courtney bit her lip. She knew she was going to regret asking, but she did anyway. "What happened at the dog park?"

"He actually wanted to play with the other dogs!" Mrs. McKenzie exploded. "That's not like him at all! He doesn't like any of his favorite toys anymore, either, but instead he's started digging out old ones that he would never touch before. I know there's something wrong with him, and it's been going on ever since I picked him up. Something must have happened to him while he was here."

"Hang on a second." Courtney poked her head into the grooming area. "Dora, I'm sure I already know the answer to this, but did anything unusual happen with Angus when he was in for his grooming appointment and hotel stay?"

Dora was busy scrubbing the dirt out of an adventurous beagle's fur, but she shook her head. "Nothing I can think of. Everything was normal. He's always good for me. Why?"

Courtney told her what was happening in the lobby.

"Beats me." Dora rolled her shoulders. "Everything was fine as far as I know."

"Thanks." She came back to the counter, where she set Angus down to look him over. There was always a chance that he had some sort of injury or sickness that his owner hadn't noticed, and that could cause him to act a little differently. "He seems perfectly fine. He doesn't seem sick or anything."

"There's *something* wrong," Mrs. McKenzie insisted. "This just isn't like him at all. Are there any harsh chemicals in the soaps or conditioners that Dora uses?"

Courtney didn't even need to consult with the groomer on this one, because she ordered all those supplies herself. "Everything is all natural. That's the way it was even before I started working here."

"There has to be something. Maybe your employees aren't being honest with you. I suggest you get to the bottom of this, Courtney, or every person I know is going to be hearing about it whether they own a dog or not!" Mrs. McKenzie banged her jade green nails on the counter.

"What's going on, Angus?" Courtney asked the dog, wishing he could answer for himself. She didn't see anything wrong with him, but behavior changes often meant that a dog was trying to tell their owner something. The last thing she wanted was for the rather loud Mrs. McKenzie to be voicing her negative opinion about the Curly Bay Pet Hotel and Rescue around town, so she had to figure something out. "I tell you what. I'll arrange for an appointment with our veterinarian, Dr. Moulton. She can look him over and help us figure this out. I can give her a call right now."

"I guess that's at least a start," Mrs. McKenzie sniffed. "I just don't like any of this. There's something going on here, and I'm going to figure out what it is!"

"Give me a second, okay?" Since Angus seemed comfortable in her arms for the moment, Courtney called the vet's office and scheduled the appointment. She looked down into the little dog's eyes, feeling sorry for him. While there was certainly some oddity to his behavior, it was also a shame that a little extra sweetness was being treated like a disease. If she couldn't work on the Tyler Lancaster case, then at least she had something else to puzzle out.

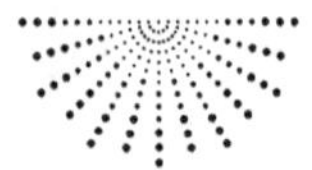

"Let's go home, sweetie." Courtney loaded Peppa into her car and headed toward the edge of town. Normally, she headed straight through the downtown area since that was the fastest way home. Instead, she cut down a few side streets to avoid it completely. She wasn't interested in driving past the grocery store and Rose's Gaming. In fact, she never had gone back in for those hamburger buns, and she just might be finding somewhere else to shop for the next few months.

It didn't matter that Detective Fletcher insisted Linda was innocent. It didn't even matter that Linda felt and acted innocent. Courtney couldn't have imagined it, and now she was stuck working in the same building with the woman until this all got sorted out. She wondered if Detective Fletcher would come bursting into the building at some point, waving an arrest warrant.

Nathan Pike waved from his porch on the house next door as she pulled up. "Long day at the office?" he called out. "I haven't seen you in a while."

"I know," Courtney sighed. She and Nathan had become close ever since she'd moved into this house. They often sat down once or twice a week before work and had coffee and doughnuts together, and sometimes they met up for dinner at one house or the other. Nathan's fluffy marmalade cat, Archie, had taken quite a liking to Peppa, and the dog seemed to feel the same way.

"I guess this past week has just been a little tough," she admitted as she walked over with an eager Peppa in tow. "I guess you might've heard about some of it."

Nathan gestured toward the empty chair next to him. "Can I get you a glass of iced tea?"

Courtney noted the waiting glass and the pitcher on the chair next to him. "It looks like you were expecting someone."

"Just you. I figured I'd pounce on you as soon as you got home and figure out why you were avoiding me," he said with a mischievous grin as he poured a glass. "Actually, I was a little bit worried about you."

Taking the glass of tea and watching as Peppa and Archie greeted each other, Courtney did her best to sum up the events of the past few days as briefly as she could. "It's all really strange," she concluded. "I know what I saw, but the police are telling me I'm wrong and now I'm spending eight hours a day with a woman who I know killed someone."

"So, what are you going to do?" Nathan asked. "And don't try to tell me you're not going to do anything, because I'm not going to believe that."

Courtney shrugged helplessly. "I understand, but I think in this case I might not actually be able to do anything. Detective Fletcher said the victim had racked up a significant amount of gambling debt, potentially with some extremely dangerous people."

"Here in Curly Bay?" Nathan asked. "I thought the mobsters and bookies stuck to the bigger cities."

"I wouldn't know," Courtney admitted. "The most I've ever done is buy a dollar scratch-off, and that's enough for me. Fletcher probably knows more than I do, though. I'd be hard-pressed to believe that someone like Linda would get wrapped up in that sort of thing, but then again it's hard to believe she was there in the first place."

"Wow. Just…wow." Nathan leaned forward and braced his elbows on his knees. "I'd like to say something that would make you feel better, but I probably can't. I'm here for you, though, if there's anything you need."

"I appreciate it." Courtney forced herself to relax into the patio chair and concentrate on just how refreshing the iced tea was. She'd thought work would be a great distraction after witnessing the murder, but that hadn't worked out so well once Linda had come back. Maybe a little bit of time with a good friend was just what she needed. "Tell me what's going on in your life."

"Actually, I did want to talk to you about that. I'm having a family gathering here at my place this weekend, and I'd like you to come." The setting sun cast golden light on his aquiline nose and strong jawline. In the right situation, he looked more like a neighborhood handyman than a web developer.

"Oh." If Courtney was looking for a diversion, then this was definitely it. The idea of meeting all of Nathan's family sounded rather intimidating. Of course, since he'd already come over and had

Thanksgiving with her and her parents, she couldn't exactly turn him down. "That sounds nice. What dish should I bring?"

"You don't have to worry about that. I already have quite a few dishes planned, and it sounds like everyone else is already bringing one or two things. We'll have more food than we can possibly use." Nathan paused. "Actually, there's one thing I need you to bring."

"Sure."

"Peppa. I'm sure Archie would be disappointed to see all the aunts and uncles but no dog. He's getting pretty attached." Nathan gestured at the two animals.

"So I see." Peppa and Archie had curled up together happily near the porch railing. Every now and then, Archie would occasionally swat at a bug or Peppa would sniff the air, but overall, the two of them seemed quite content with their current situation.

Nathan gestured with his thumb toward the front door. "Do you want to stay for dinner?"

"No, I really shouldn't. I have…" Courtney trailed off as Peppa stood up and made a beeline right for

Nathan's door. She stood there waiting for someone to open it, her tail wagging.

"I think Peppa's made her mind up for you. Come on in. I've got a chicken roasting."

An hour later and with her stomach quite full, Courtney headed back over to her house. She flicked on the lights and went through her typical evening routine, but her body was moving on autopilot. Her mind was too busy with thoughts of Linda. She'd managed to let it all go for a little bit while she sat at Nathan's kitchen table to enjoy herb-roasted chicken, baked potatoes, and asparagus. It'd been a wonderful little escape, and she was glad he'd stopped her as she'd gotten home, but no matter how good of a dinner she had, she wasn't going to be able to just forget about that night in front of Rose's Gaming.

"I know I saw her," she said out loud to Peppa as she put a load of towels in the washing machine. "I couldn't have just made it up."

The dog offered little help, merely supervising her owner as she did her chores.

"You know what, even if I don't actually work the case, there's nothing saying I can't do a little research on the internet. Right?" Courtney headed into the living room and grabbed her laptop.

Peppa laid down on the floor in front of the couch and rested her head on Courtney's foot.

It was a comforting weight. Courtney had known she'd made the right decision in adopting Peppa, and not only because the dog had saved her life once. It was nice to know that someone was always there with her, and Courtney knew she was quite privileged in being able to take her companion to work with her. She only wished she could focus a little more on the tranquility and contentment she could get from the dog as she pulled up her browser.

The first several stories that her search returned were from several news outlets. They glossed over the general events of that fateful night, and though each of them phrased the story a bit differently, they all essentially said the same thing. One suspect had been apprehended but let go, and the police were still searching for the real killer. Courtney read over each one carefully, looking for any detail she might have missed that could be important. She found nothing.

"Well, that's no help. Let's see what else we can dig up on him."

Peppa didn't answer, and she had begun to snore.

There were some of the typical links that invited her to look at Tyler's social media account. Courtney dared to click on them, hoping beyond hope that she might find something that would give her some hint she hadn't thought of before. Unfortunately, Tyler's accounts were set so that only those he'd already accepted as friends could see his information. She could see nothing more than his profile picture. In one, he stood in front of a brightly lit casino, probably in Las Vegas or Reno, with his hands held wide and a big smile on his face.

"Again, no help," she mumbled as she moved along.

Courtney was beginning to lose hope as the search results showed her less and became more obscure. She was just about to exit her browser and shut her computer down for the night when something caught her eye. It was from the *Ruby Cove Chronicle*, the newspaper from the next town. Courtney clicked on the link and held her breath as she studied the article that pulled up.

Sherman-Lancaster Wedding was written across the top of the page. There was a photo underneath, with the caption detailing only where and when the wedding had taken place. There was little information, but Courtney knew that people didn't put their engagement and wedding announcements in the paper like they used to.

What was more interesting anyway was the photo itself. It portrayed Tyler Lancaster, smiling at the camera and wearing a nice suit. He looked simply like a younger, slightly slimmer version of the man she'd seen in his social media profiles. There was nothing unusual there. The bride was listed as Ann Sherman. Courtney blinked and looked away from the screen, starting to wonder if she really was going crazy. She had to be. When she looked back, she still saw the same image of a bride in a tea-length cream dress, with a sweet smile on her face and a bouquet of pink peonies.

The woman in the wedding dress next to Tyler Lancaster was Linda.

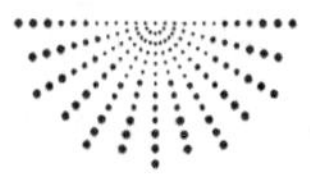

The next day, Courtney drummed her fingers on the steering wheel as she headed over to Dr. Moulton's office. She'd gotten up that morning at her normal time, and she'd done her normal routine. After giving Peppa a chance to go outside, she showered and came out of the bathroom to the wonderful scent of coffee brewing. There was something almost luxurious about a simple thing like a coffee pot with a timer on it. After breakfast and getting ready, she moved through the typical morning traffic to work.

Through all of it, she hadn't been able to stop thinking about Linda. Seeing her in real life when she showed up shortly after opening didn't make things any easier. Courtney had done her best to get through the first part of the day until the vet appointment, but there were now more questions than answers. Why was Linda the bride in Tyler Lancaster's wedding photo? And if her husband was already dead, as she'd claimed on her first day at the shelter, then why would she have shown up at Rose's Gaming to kill Tyler? Was she having an affair, and she finally ended up killing both of them? Nobody had ever said how Linda's husband had died, other than that it was sudden.

And then there was the question of whether Linda knew Courtney was a witness to the murder. That part bothered her the most, because she had no idea if her temporary coworker was now plotting a way to get rid of her, too.

In that sense, it was nice to have a chance to get away from the office—and from Linda—while she went to Dr. Moulton's office. Courtney had to leave Peppa behind, but her dog was hanging out with Dora and making friends with a Bassett hound that'd come in for a bath.

Just as Courtney pulled into the parking lot, a massive white SUV swung in behind her and came to a hard halt just in front of the building. The windows were tinted too darkly for Courtney to tell if it was Mrs. McKenzie, and the car simply sat there running for a moment. It wasn't until Courtney had gotten all the way up to the door that Mrs. McKenzie finally stepped out with Angus in her arms.

"Good morning," Courtney said as she opened the door.

The middle of Mrs. McKenzie's mouth pushed up toward her nose in a deep, frowny pout. Her large designer sunglasses were just as dark as the windows on her vehicle, so Courtney couldn't see her eyes. She didn't need to, because her voice said it all. "We'll see about that," she snapped.

The receptionist had them sit down to wait. Courtney positioned herself near a large tank full of tropical fish, but she couldn't be diverted by the bright colors for long. She was now too worried about how this appointment would go. What if the vet did find something wrong with Angus? What if it was the shelter's fault? She was already rather preoccupied by a very strange murder case, and she didn't want to have to scramble to save the PR of the company.

An assistant appeared in the doorway at the back of the room and checked her clipboard. "Angus?"

The three of them piled into an exam room. Normally, the assistant would check the dog's weight, temperature, and heartbeat. Since Courtney had already explained the unusual situation over the phone, she merely got them settled in before promising that the doctor would be in soon.

If Courtney thought it'd been awkward out in the waiting room, this was much worse. Mrs. McKenzie sat primly in the sole chair. Angus curled up her lap and shoved his face against the front of her pale blue blazer. He shed little dark hairs across the thighs of her bright white pants. Mrs. McKenzie had her shoulders back and her chin out, looking stubborn and determined. She'd flipped her sunglasses up on top of her head, and there was some softness in her eyes as she scratched the dog's chin. "Don't worry, sweet one. We'll figure this out and get you back to rights." Her eyes hardened again when she glared at Courtney.

There was little Courtney could say to convince her that she hadn't done anything wrong, and so she waited.

"Good morning!" Dr. Moulton called out brightly as she came in the room. "Let's put the little guy up here on the table and see what we can figure out."

"There's definitely something wrong," Mrs. McKenzie declared as she gently placed the dog on the exam table. "He's constantly following me around, which just isn't like him. He wants to be next to me twenty-four-seven. It's like he's trying to tell me he doesn't feel good."

"Well, we'll find out. Isn't that right, sugar?" Dr. Moulton smiled down at the dog as she took his vitals. "Has he been eating normally?"

"He's eating, but not normally," Mrs. McKenzie retorted. "He usually takes one dainty little bite at a time, like a gentleman. Now he scoops big mouthfuls of kibble, carries them across the room to the corner, drops it all, and then eats each piece before going back for more. It's very bizarre."

"I've known other dogs who do eat that way," the vet pointed out, "but I do agree it's an unusual habit for him to start suddenly. Has he been through any sort of trauma?"

"That's exactly what I'm trying to find out, isn't it?" Mrs. McKenzie stomped a sandal the color of a robin's egg against the linoleum, startling the dog.

Dr. Moulton shot Courtney a meaningful glance across the table, and one eyebrow quirked slightly. Courtney knew they would be talking about this one later. "Yes," she said out loud, "let's see what we can figure out."

After a thorough physical exam, the vet had blood drawn for a full workup. Angus was taken by the doctor and an assistant into an adjoining room for some x-rays. Mrs. McKenzie insisted on accompanying them, which meant she had to let the vet tech drape her in a heavy vest. Courtney amused herself a little by noticing that the dark gray didn't coordinate with the rest of her outfit, but she was a little sorry for the staff at having to deal with her.

It felt like it was taking forever, and the steady tick of the wall clock didn't help. It just reminded Courtney of how much time she was spending here, away from the office, simply because Mrs. McKenzie wanted to put the blame on her. She desperately hoped there was no good reason for it. She'd never do anything to harm an animal, at least not on purpose.

Finally, Dr. Moulton looked at them both and sighed. "Ladies, I'm afraid you're seeing all of this as I am, and I think you can come to the same conclusion that I can. The bloodwork is all completely normal. The x-rays didn't turn up anything. He's eating and drinking, and he's using the bathroom. I don't see anything that indicates an allergic reaction to anything he ate or was otherwise exposed to. There's no sign of abuse. Angus is in perfect health."

"But that can't be right!" Mrs. McKenzie scooped her dog up off the table and cradled him delicately in her arms. He reached up and licked her under the chin. "See? He never would've done that before! There's definitely something wrong."

"I'm sorry, but whatever is happening with him must be psychological. I agree with you that dogs often change their behavior to tell us when they're not feeling well, but that doesn't necessarily mean it's physical. Maybe he's just craving some extra attention," Dr. Moulton explained.

As though Angus could understand exactly what the vet was saying, he flopped against his owner's chest and rubbed his cheek against her shirt. Courtney frowned. She didn't want Dr. Moulton to find anything wrong with Angus, especially if there was any chance that the shelter was responsible. Still, she knew that Angus was usually far more aloof than that. If he were a child, she'd think he was acting up just to get attention.

Mrs. McKenzie was sweet and gentle as she handled her dog, but her eyes shot daggers as she glared at both Courtney and Dr. Moulton. "Don't think I don't see what's going on here. You work with the shelter all the time," she said to the vet. "And you paid her to say what you wanted!" she accused Courtney.

While anger flared in Courtney's chest and threatened to break her resolve, Dr. Moulton remained professional. "Mrs. McKenzie, you've been right here through the entire exam. I showed you the bloodwork results as well as the x-rays, and I explained them all. I'd even be happy to give you copies. I'm quite confident that there's nothing physically wrong with Angus."

"I'll take those copies, and I'll take Angus straight over to my own vet. We'll have to see what he says about this. You should be prepared to hear from my lawyer!" Mrs. McKenzie turned and stormed from the room. The effect was only slightly dampened by the way she tipped her head down so she could rest her cheek against the top of her dog's head.

"That was interesting," Dr. Moulton said quietly. They could both hear Mrs. McKenzie speaking loudly to the receptionist about Angus's records. "You can wipe that look off your face, though. You don't have anything to worry about."

"I'm glad you believe that. I just wish she did." Courtney pressed her hand over her eyes for a moment, realizing just how tired she was. She hadn't been sleeping all that well. "I know that we take the absolute best care possible of all the animals that we're responsible for, whether they're a paid client or a rescue off the streets. It's really frustrating."

"Mrs. McKenzie is the one who's going to be frustrated as she tries to figure out how to construct a lawsuit against either one of us. I don't think most people would complain about a dog who's suddenly sweeter than he used to be." Dr. Moulton shook her head, making her dark ponytail sway against the back of her lab coat. "There's nothing wrong at all with that dog, other than maybe his haircut."

Courtney laughed, and it echoed in the small room. "I can't say it's my favorite, either, but everyone in town has been asking Dora for it."

"Just one of those trendy things," the vet acknowledged. "Hang in there, Courtney. I know you do good work, and no matter how expensive of a lawyer she gets, she won't be able to touch you."

Courtney hoped she was right.

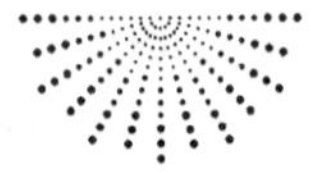

CHAPTER NINE

The rest of the day dragged on, and by the time Courtney finally got off work she was completely exhausted. She'd jumped every time the phone rang or someone walked through the door, thoroughly expecting Mrs. McKenzie to have already found a way to sic her lawyers on her. Then there was the fact that she had to interact with Linda nearly the entire time she was at the office. Murderer or not, the woman wasn't Dora or Jessi's problem. She was hers. And so, Courtney had kept herself in charge of Linda, keeping an eye on her progress and ensuring that she had a task waiting for her as soon as the previous one was finished. That meant, of course, that she also had to go in behind her and fix all the mistakes she was still making.

As she and Peppa headed home, Courtney was so distracted by her thoughts that she forgot to turn off before she hit the downtown area. Her stomach swirled as she stopped at a red light, realizing that she was already less than a block away from Rose's Gaming and the grocery store. She grimaced as she tried to decide if she should make a last-minute turn and swing down an alley to avoid the area, or if she should push forward. Courtney looked to Peppa in the passenger seat. When she saw that her dog wasn't the least bit affected, she decided she should go on. She often used Peppa as a gauge for situations, and she hadn't been wrong yet.

The light turned green, and she rolled forward. The next thing Courtney knew, she was flicking on her turn signal and pulling into the grocery store's parking lot. From what she could tell, she was in the exact same spot where she'd been parked that fateful night. It all looked about the same as it had then. The bright pink sign above Rose's shone down onto the asphalt, and the welcoming glow of the grocery store welcomed all those who needed to fill their fridges and pantries.

Slowly, Courtney's fingers wrapped around the door handle. She got out and just stood there for a moment, staring at the scene. If she hadn't been there to see it herself, she'd never have thought anything like that would've happened. How easily a tragic event could be erased. It hadn't been erased in her mind, though. Courtney could still see it all clear as day, and Linda was still the person holding the gun.

It was frustrating that there was so little information to go on. Even if she was going to pursue this case, she had no place to start. Courtney already knew who the killer was, but she had no way to prove it. Detective Fletcher had mentioned that this might have been some sort of vendetta over gambling debts, but Courtney had no idea who in Curly Bay might possibly have anything to do with that.

Then she realized as she stood there, maybe she did know someone. With a quiet command to Peppa to stay in the car, and seeing that Peppa was perfectly content, she headed into Rose's Gaming.

The interior of the video gaming parlor was long and low. The lighting mostly came from the bright flashes of the digital slot machines that lined each side of the narrow room, each of them advertising the big winnings that were possible if one only sat down and gave it a try. Courtney saw that some of them were themed after popular TV shows or comic book characters, while others sported cats or fruit.

Several of the machines were occupied, but she wasn't here to gamble. She moved toward the back, where a familiar man stood behind a counter selling snacks and drinks.

Recognition lit up his face when he looked up from restocking some Fritos and saw her. "Hey, there! I've been thinking about you off and on since the other night. I was hoping you were doing all right."

"I'm hanging on. I want to tell you how much I appreciate what you did for me. You were very kind." A cold bottle of water and a few kind words might not be much, but she really had been grateful. This man was a stranger, and he'd had no obligation.

"Not a problem at all. You here for a little bit of gaming?" He gestured toward the blinking machines.

"No, I just wanted to talk to you for a minute if I could."

Concern crossed his face, but he nodded. "It's a bit loud in here. We can step outside."

"That'd be great." The air was hot and humid on her face after being in the frigid air conditioning of Rose's, but she didn't mind. It was nice to get away from the noise. "I'm going to just get my dog out of my car if that's all right with you."

"Sure, I love dogs." He even squatted down and held his hand out for Peppa to sniff when they returned a moment later, and she deemed him worthy of petting her.

She had to figure out some way to start this conversation, but she was concerned it was going to be awkward no matter how she went about it. "I guess I should introduce myself. I'm Courtney Cain."

"Jake Bell. I own this place." He continued to pet Peppa as he spoke. "What can I do for you?"

She bit her lip . "I know this is going to sound kind of weird, but I was wondering if there's anything you know about the man who was shot here."

His dark eyes narrowed at her slightly, but in more of a curious way than an unfriendly one. "I didn't think you were with the police force."

"I can't blame you, considering the way I reacted to all that. And you're right; I'm not. I'm just a curious citizen who wants to see justice done. I'm disturbed by what I saw here the other night, to say the least. In fact, I'm starting to wonder if I'm ever going to be able to stop thinking about it." Courtney purposely kept her eyes away from the alley, not wanting that image of Linda to be any clearer in her head than it already was.

"I can understand that. It's not been the easiest on me, either. I never thought of Curly Bay as the sort of place where things like that happen. It might be nice to talk to someone who understands."

A small amount of relief washed over Courtney, but it wasn't enough to undo the knots of tension that'd been building up in her shoulders. Jake could've easily told her she was nuts for wanting to find out any further information and told her to leave him alone. "Yeah, I was thinking so."

"Well, I can't say that I knew Tyler personally. Not really. He came in all the time, and he often spent an hour or two here. He won a little bit, but he lost a lot just like everyone else." Jake thumbed over his shoulder at his establishment.

"Was there anything unusual going on with him that night?" She might as well ask. It couldn't hurt.

He lifted a shoulder. "Not that I'm aware of. He was texting on his cell phone a lot while he was playing, but that was pretty normal. He told me his old lady was always nagging at him to come home and how she didn't want him to have a little fun."

"Does that sort of thing happen to your customers a lot?" Courtney thought it was interesting that Tyler was being nagged by his wife or girlfriend right before being shot by a woman, regardless of whether it was Linda or someone else.

Jack rolled his hand through the air. "Everyone is a little bit different. Sometimes we get husbands and wives that come in together, even. It's nothing that I found particularly notable other than the fact that Tyler would tell me about it. This isn't a bar, but occasionally people treat it that way and they want to talk."

"Someone told me that Lancaster had racked up a lot of gambling debt. Do you know anything about that?"

"No way." Jack put his hands up in the air and shook his head. "They put money in the machines, and they get whatever they win back out of them. Nobody ever owes me anything, and I don't know about places or people like that."

"Okay." Courtney nodded. The gambling debt was a dead end for the moment, but it was interesting that Tyler Lancaster was constantly complaining about his 'old lady.' It supported her theory that Linda was having an affair, but it didn't prove anything. "Thanks for taking the time to talk to me. I feel a little better."

"Anytime. Stop by if you feel the need."

When Jack had gone back inside and Courtney had climbed back into her car, she knew there was one source of information she hadn't yet explored. She called her boss.

"Is everything all right?" Ms. O'Donnell said when she answered the phone.

"Yes. I'm sorry for the odd hour. Everything is closed and secure at the shelter. I just had a few questions for you about Linda."

Ms. O'Donnell sighed. "Is she still so hard to get along with?"

"No. I get along with her fine, but she's difficult to work with. I was wondering if she might need to do something else to get herself back on track. I know her husband's death has been hard on her, and I think she might be having an even harder time now that she's been accused of murder." She held her breath, wondering if Linda had told her friend about the incident.

"Oh, that," Ms. O'Donnell said dismissively. "I'm always saying we need to get some new officers hired, because some of the ones we have now are old and blind! Linda would never do something as drastic as that, no matter what the circumstances were."

"Were things…all right between Linda and her husband before he passed away? Were they having any issues? I only ask because I want to make sure I understand where Linda is coming from, so I can help her as much as possible. I'm not a therapist or anything, but I am working with her all day." Courtney glanced at Peppa for strength, but the dog was leaning against the window and was almost asleep.

"I think it might've been easier on her if they'd had some sort of trouble, but they were perfect soul mates. When Kevin had a heart attack, it really devastated her. She cried like crazy at the funeral, and that was after he'd already been gone a week. I'd have thought her tears had already run out. And the poor thing hardly had anybody to lean on but me." Ms. O'Donnell sounded genuinely upset by this.

"She didn't have any family?" Courtney pressed.

"No, or at least not that she could count on. She pulled herself away from them quite some time ago because they were always causing such trouble. I'll put it to you like this: Linda has a sister, and even though I've known Linda for about ten years, I've never met her."

"Wow." Courtney felt genuinely bad for Linda. If she could put aside what she'd seen here a few nights ago, she'd probably be a lot more understanding of Linda's predicament and how hard her life was on her right now. It would be so difficult to lose a husband, but then to have none of her family at her side? "That's terrible. I'm glad at least you could be there for her."

"Me, too. I've got to get going, dear. Please do be patient with Linda. She's trying her best."

"I know." When they'd hung up, Courtney started up the car and headed home. There were a few clues in place, but none of them seemed to be leading anywhere.

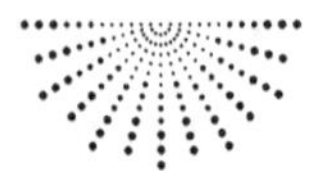

CHAPTER TEN

"I thought I told you not to bring anything," Nathan said when Courtney showed up on Saturday.

His driveway was packed with cars, and there seemed to be people everywhere. Apparently the Pike clan was rather large, as there were people seated on the porch and inside the house. Several children were running around as well.

Courtney shrugged as she handed him the pan of brownies. "I couldn't just show up empty-handed. Besides, it was kind of nice to spend a bit of time in the kitchen

"Come on in. We'll put this on the table, and I'll introduce you to everyone."

Stepping into the house, Courtney was instantly overwhelmed by a gaggle of older ladies.

"You must be Courtney!"

"It's so nice to meet you."

"We've heard a lot about you."

Courtney felt a flush of embarrassment over her cheeks, and she saw a similar one on Nathan's as he cleared his throat.

"Um, Courtney, this is my Grandma Lorraine. My great-aunts Charlene and Margaret."

They all shook hands and fawned over her some more, asking questions about what she did for a living, how long she'd been doing that, and when she was planning to settle down and have children. It was all very sweet, and Courtney was glad that they were so willing to welcome them to their family gathering when she was just a neighbor, but she could see her own discomfort growing just as Nathan's was. In fact, she was jealous of Peppa, who found Archie and was playing with him in the corner.

After a few minutes, Nathan jumped back into the conversation. "I still have some other people I'd like

Courtney to meet. If you'll excuse us." He guided her toward the back door.

Archie and Peppa followed them as they moved onto the back porch. It was also crowded with people, but Nathan brought her down into the yard and to some lawn chairs parked under the shade trees. "I'm really sorry about that," he said, barely able to meet her eyes. "I'm afraid my grandma and my aunts have some rather old-fashioned ideas."

"It's all right. Really." Courtney knew that she and Nathan had some possibility of being more than friends, but neither one of them wanted to push it. They were content with spending time together and getting to know each other. "They seem very nice."

"And you seem like you might still be a little stressed," Nathan noted.

The apprehensive look on his face was so sweet. It was nice to know he was so concerned. "Yeah, you could say that. I guess I'm just one of those people who likes to know the answers. I don't want to keep guessing and wondering. In this case, I might have to settle for never knowing."

"The police haven't made any breakthroughs?" he asked as he watched the dog and the cat chase each other around the back yard.

"If they have, they haven't told me about it. I think Detective Fletcher would tell me, too, since he was so concerned about keeping me out of this case." She was just about to tell him about her visit to Rose's Gaming when a young boy about ten years old ran up to them.

"Is that your dog?" he asked excitedly. He had dark red hair and a smattering of freckles over his cheeks. He twisted the hem of his Denver Broncos shirt with one hand and carried a Solo cup of soda in the other.

"Logan, this is my friend Courtney. She lives next door," Nathan said politely. "Courtney, this is my nephew, Logan."

"It's nice to meet you," she said with a smile. He was a cute kid, and she instantly clicked with anybody who could get that excited about dogs. She whistled to Peppa, who came running over with Archie at his heels. "And yes, this is my dog. Her name is Peppa."

Logan started to reach out toward her, but he pulled his hand back. "Sorry. Can I pet her?" he corrected himself.

"You sure can. She loves attention."

Peppa proved the point as she panted happily while Logan petted her head. She bumped him with her nose when he stopped, prompting a giggle from Logan.

"Can I play with her?" His eyes were bright with excitement.

"Of course. Just so you know, she does get a little bit hyper when she's around kids. It's just because she's really happy, though."

"Hey, Peppa. You wanna play?" Logan asked, patting his thigh. "I think I can find a ball. We can run around and play!"

Peppa was just as excited as he was, and Logan was getting her even more riled. Her big paws landed on his thighs, making him stumble backwards. Logan's soda sloshed up out of his cup and all down the front of his shirt.

"Oh no! I'm so sorry!" Courtney exclaimed. She grabbed Peppa's collar. It hadn't been the dog's fault, of course, but she didn't want her jump up again.

Logan looked down at the saturated Broncos logo and shrugged. "That's okay. My mom always makes me bring an extra outfit with me. I'll just go change." He ran into the house.

"I'm really sorry about that," Courtney said to Nathan, embarrassed all over again.

"He's fine, and he was the one encouraging Peppa. Kids are tough."

The two of them descended into conversation on their own, with Nathan discussing some of his current website projects and Courtney going over what little she'd found out about Tyler Lancaster. A few minutes later, Logan showed up again. This time, he was wearing a Chicago Bears shirt.

"You got changed quickly," Courtney remarked with a smile. "I'm sure Peppa is ready to play now."

The boy looked at her with confusion. "Huh?"

"Courtney, this is Landon. He's Logan's twin brother."

"Oh. Oh, no. I'm so sorry. I had no idea." She was starting to wish she hadn't accepted Nathan's invitation or that she'd had some other plans. Courtney enjoyed spending time with Nathan, and she was glad to meet his family, but she'd been humiliated way too many times for one day.

"It's all right," Landon replied easily. "Can I play with your dog?"

"Sure."

Landon and Peppa took off across the yard, and Logan showed up to join them a minute later. He was now wearing a striped t-shirt instead of the Broncos one.

"If it weren't for their clothing, I wouldn't be able to tell them apart at all," Courtney said quietly to Nathan. "I feel so bad!"

"Don't," he assured her. "This happens with them all the time. They even had to wear nametags at school when they were younger. My sister is just lucky that they're good kids, and they don't use it to their advantage. At least, not yet. I'm being rude. Let me get you something to drink."

Courtney settled in to chat with Nathan and watch the kids play, happy to lose herself in a pretty afternoon with good company.

CHAPTER ELEVEN

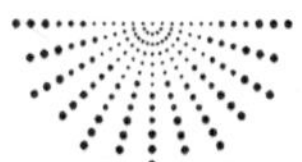

By the time the party wound down and Courtney headed home with a happily exhausted Peppa in tow, she was feeling better than she had in a week. She'd not only chatted with Nathan but with all the rest of his family that he'd ended up introducing her to. The Pikes were a wonderful bunch, and they'd all been welcoming and kind.

Courtney checked that Peppa had plenty of food and water before she sat down and turned on the TV. She didn't have any major plans for the rest of the day, and she mindlessly flicked through a few channels. She felt restless, and even though she should feel perfectly satisfied after such a nice afternoon, her mind began churning once again. She felt as though something had occurred to her and then the thought had disappeared, sort of like she'd gone to the store for something specific but then couldn't remember what it was. Courtney ran back over her day. Though chatting with the older ladies certainly stood out, so did the incident with Logan and Landon.

She realized a few minutes later that she was thinking so much about this that she was only staring blankly at the screen. Courtney flicked off the TV and picked up her cell phone.

"Curly Bay Public Library. This is Lisa. How can I help you?"

"Hey. It's Courtney. I know you guys are getting ready to close in a little bit, but I was wondering if you'd be willing to stick around and help me out with some research. Don't feel obligated if you're busy," she added quickly.

"Is this the kind of research I think it might be?" Lisa asked curiously, "because I'm always up for that."

"Then I'll be there as soon as I can." Courtney hung up and put her shoes back on. "I'll have to leave you here, sweetheart," she said to Peppa.

Wiped out from all her playtime with Logan and Landon, Peppa merely lifted her head, blinked at Courtney sleepily, and laid back down again.

The last library patrons were just leaving as Courtney pulled up and trotted inside. "Hey. I hope I'm not keeping you too late."

"Not at all." Lisa brushed a bit of her curly hair behind her ear as she finished straightening up her desk for the day. "I told the others they could head out and I would lock up behind them. I didn't want to shut anything down until I knew what you needed."

Courtney leaned on the counter on the front of the circulation desk. "I'm not sure myself, but maybe you do. I'm trying to figure out if my new volunteer is a murderer or not."

Lisa's eyebrows shot up. "Tell me more. I've got all evening."

She gave Lisa the basic rundown of what had happened. "I can't believe I hadn't called you and told you about all this before. It's just been such a crazy and stressful week. I guess part of it is because Detective Fletcher told me to stay out of it, and I knew if you and I got to talking, then I'd cross that line."

"Sounds to me like you were already starting to do that," Lisa said with a wink as they headed toward a room near the back of the building. This was where all the microfiche was stored that held everything that wasn't already digitized. There were microfiche machines as well as a couple of computers.

"I guess that's true, considering my little trip to Rose's Gaming. It felt like a big clue that Tyler's wife was bothering him about gambling, but that still doesn't explain why it was Linda who killed him. And I know Detective Fletcher insists that it wasn't Linda, but I can't be crazy, Lisa. I know what I saw." She felt a sense of desperation wash over her once again.

"So, what can we do?" Lisa asked helpfully. "Where should we start?"

"I already dug around online to see if there was anything I could find on Tyler. I found a wedding photo, and the bride looked just like Linda, but it wasn't. I guess let's start with Linda."

"All right. Let's see what we can find between the internet and the microfiche. What's her name?"

"Linda Nicholson. Linda Wheeler Nicholson, actually. She told me Wheeler is her maiden name, so hopefully that helps. I'll let you do the microfiche.

You're better at it." Courtney sat down in front of the computer.

"I guess I should be, considering what I do for a living," Lisa said with a little laugh.

Courtney tapped away at the keyboard. At least when it came to the internet, there was plenty she could've done on her own. It was more fun, however, to have someone else at her side. It didn't take long for a very recent search result to pop up. "I found an article about her husband's death."

"Anything that doesn't line up?" Lisa asked as she rifled through a file drawer.

"No, not so far." Courtney looked carefully through each line of text. It was a simple little tidbit about Kevin's sudden heart attack and where the funeral would be held, but any slight detail that didn't line up with Linda's side of the story could serve as a clue. There was no indication that anything was out of the ordinary.

"Okay. I pulled up her name in the files, and it looks like there are some older articles about her when she was still Wheeler. I'd say these are probably from when she was a little girl, so it might not be anything more exciting than a spelling bee or an art contest."

"Hey, you never know. I'd like to see them when you get them pulled up." Courtney continued to shuffle through social media profiles she couldn't access as well as paid sites offering criminal background checks. None of it was doing her any good so far, and she started to wonder if she and Lisa would find anything. The media could be helpful at dropping clues, but Courtney's mind wandered off as she tried to think of other ways to get more information.

She daydreamed about what it might be like to just corner Linda and ask her outright. Courtney was sure Linda would deny the allegations, but would she reveal some other truth? Or perhaps she would simply throw her chin in the air, admit what she'd done and how she'd covered it up, and ask Courtney just what she thought she'd be able to do about it. After all, the police already believed her alibi.

"Okay, here's the first one."

Lisa's voice interrupted her thoughts. Courtney got up and came over to the microfiche just as Lisa brought the old photo into focus. It was titled "Twin Day at Curly Bay Elementary" and showed two rows of children. They were paired off and dressed alike.

"Probably Spirit Week or something," Lisa murmured. "They're so cute. Look at these two boys. They both wore their Superman t-shirts."

Courtney skimmed the caption underneath the photo, looking for Linda's name. She found it and matched it up with a little blonde girl in the front row, smiling and wearing a flowered dress. The girl next to her was also blonde and wearing the same dress, and both had styled their hair in pigtails. Courtney checked the caption for the other girl's name, and then she found herself checking and double-checking what she saw. It might have been obvious if this was a newer photograph, one that hadn't been taken with an old camera and then printed in the low resolution of a newspaper.

"Linda and Ann Wheeler," Courtney said quietly. "Linda has a twin?"

"It sure looks like it to me," Lisa agreed. "I'll bet we can double check that, just to make sure this isn't a cousin or a sister that's close in age. Do you know Linda's date of birth?"

Courtney tapped a finger against her forehead as she tried to think. "I can't say that I paid much attention to that when I was putting it all in the system. I couldn't tell you exactly, but I think I know the year."

"That's a start," Lisa said, just as positive and chipper as when they'd started. "We know her last name, so it should be easy enough to scan through the babies born for the year in Curly Bay. That is, provided they were born in Curly Bay. A lot of people around here seem to stay in town their whole lives, and since she went to school here, I'd say it's likely. There's always a possibility that the Wheeler girls are a transplant from somewhere else, though."

"Ann must be the woman I found in Tyler Lancaster's wedding photo," Courtney reasoned. "She had a different last name, though, so that was what threw me off initially. Tyler and Ann got married in Ruby Cove, so that might be the place to check if our local files don't turn anything up."

"Here we go." Lisa had already found the film roll she was looking for and had fished it out of a drawer.

"You know, you work awfully quickly. You might be wasting your talents here at a little small-town library," Courtney said with a wry smile.

"I'm just a big fish in a little pond." Lisa was smiling, too. "Besides, if I went somewhere else, I'd never have met you. Whatever I would've ended up using my research skills on, I'm sure it wouldn't be nearly as fun."

Courtney held her breath as Lisa found the birth announcement. "Kenneth and Denise Wheeler proudly announce the birth of twin daughters Linda and Ann," she read aloud. "How about that? Linda has a twin. It's such a simple solution, but I didn't see it right in front of me until I met Nathan's twin nephews today. I couldn't tell them apart at all, not even when they were both standing right in front of me and wearing completely different shirts. I'll have to call Detective Fletcher."

Lisa was already up and out of her seat, looking through files and drawers again. "Are you sure you want to do that? I mean, he told you to stay out of the case."

"I can't just let it go," Courtney reasoned. "This will not only completely clear Linda's name and eliminate any doubt as to her innocence but also make sure justice is served to the real killer."

"No, but I'm sure we could find a way to get him the information anonymously," Lisa pointed out.

Courtney gave that a moment of thought and then shook her head. "Probably, but he trusts me to be honest with him. Or at least, mostly honest. I think

I'd rather just tell him. What are you doing, anyway? We've already got this figured out."

"You know how when you're doing a jigsaw puzzle and you get to put the very last piece in, and you just sort of smooth your fingers over the whole thing and savor all that work you've done."

"It's been a while since I've done a jigsaw, but yeah."

"That's what I'm doing. You said Ann's last name was Sherman when she married Tyler Lancaster. I've already got a good idea of why she wasn't listed as Wheeler, but I figured it was worth checking out." She quickly loaded up the next round of film. "Ann was married before to a Ted Sherman. Here's the divorce announcement."

"You're too good, Lisa." Courtney dialed Detective Fletcher.

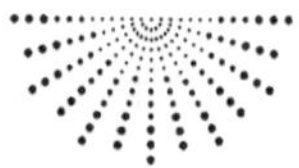

CHAPTER TWELVE

"Courtney, we've got a bit of a problem."

Courtney looked up at Linda with a smile on her face. She felt horrible for thinking Linda was a murderer, but she was thrilled to know she wasn't. There couldn't be any problem in the world as difficult as the one that had just been solved, even if it was Monday. "What's that?"

"A couple came in and asked to have a look at Bruce. They saw him online and were thinking about adopting him, but he was horribly mean during their visit. He stayed on the other side of the room and didn't want to have anything to do with them. When the man tried to reach out and pet him, I thought Bruce might bite!"

"That *is* a problem," Courtney agreed. "It's strange, because he seemed so sweet when he came in. Some dogs don't react well to being stuck in a shelter." She looked up when she saw movement through the front glass door. "Oh, boy. Here comes trouble."

Mrs. McKenzie burst in the door, holding Angus as usual. Today she was dressed head-to-toe in a buttery yellow. The woman was keen on coordinates. "Courtney, I've about had it! *Something* happened to my dog while he was here. I don't know what it is, and neither does your vet or mine, apparently. That doesn't mean I'm just going to give up. Until someone comes forward and tells me the truth, I'm going to make it my mission to let everyone in Curly Bay know exactly what kind of operation you have going on here!"

Courtney set down her pen. She was working on just the right response, one that would put Mrs. McKenzie in her place without being unprofessional, when she glanced at Angus. The information she'd discovered at the library two days ago was still fresh in her mind, and she suddenly realized there was yet another case of mistaken identity. "Linda, could you get Jessi and Dora in here for me?"

"Oh, going to gang up on me now?" Mrs. McKenzie snapped.

"Not at all. Just bear with me." Courtney waited until her other two workers had returned, and then she whispered another request to Linda before turning back to Jessi, Dora, and Mrs. McKenzie. "Dora, how would you normally describe Angus's personality?"

The groomer looked at her quizzically, but she didn't question her. "He's excellent to work with on the grooming table, but he's not exactly what I'd call a friendly dog. He doesn't want any extra hugs or pets, nor does he need comforting. He's just very austere. No offense, Mrs. McKenzie."

"None taken."

"But now Angus is the complete opposite. And Jessi." Courtney turned to her shelter worker. "Last week we took in a dog named Bruce. How would you describe his personality when he was first taken in?"

"An absolute doll," Jessi replied easily. "I think he's having a tough time with being in a kennel, though. He's not really like that anymore."

Just then, Linda came to the lobby with Bruce, just as Courtney had asked. "I invite all of you take a look at these two dogs and tell me which is which."

Stunned silence took over as all four of them looked from Angus to Bruce and back again.

Linda put a hand over her mouth, her eyes wide. "Oh, no."

"They could be stunt doubles," Jessi giggled.

Dora looked like she was going to be sick.

Even Mrs. McKenzie was squinting. "They look exactly alike," she murmured. "I can't even tell the difference. It's like they were cut from the same cloth."

Courtney allowed herself an ironic smile as she wondered if that cloth would be butter yellow, pale blue, jade green, or baby pink. "Mrs. McKenzie, please hand your dog to Dora. Linda, put Bruce on the floor."

With the scene set, Courtney waited anxiously. The dog Linda had brought over from the kennel marched over to Mrs. McKenzie, dropped his hind end to the floor, and stared up at her expectantly.

"My baby! My baby Angus! Oh, Mommy missed you so much!" She scooped him up.

Angus braced his front paws against the daffodil-colored dress to keep her from hugging him too tightly, and he turned his head slightly away when she tried to kiss him.

"I think what happened here is that both Bruce and Angus were in for grooming at the same time. As you can all see, they look exactly alike, especially with identical haircuts. One went to the shelter side, and one to the hotel side, but they got mixed up in the process," Courtney reasoned.

"Oh, thank goodness! Oh, my baby! There's nothing wrong with you at all, you wonderful, mean little man. Come on, sweetie. Let's go home!" Mrs. McKenzie turned to the door, but she paused and looked over her shoulder. "I'm sorry, Courtney."

"Me, too," Courtney replied genuinely, breathing a sigh of relief.

"Um, Courtney," Linda said quietly when their client was gone. "Could I talk to you for a minute?"

"Absolutely." Courtney guided her back into the office, where they sat down at her desk.

"I want to apologize," Linda said immediately. "I think I may have been the one who mixed the dogs up. I've been mixing up a lot of things here lately, and I know that's made things difficult for all of you.

My intentions were good, but perhaps I should've found a better way to occupy my time."

"Linda, it's all right. I should apologize to you for any frustration I've shown to you. You're going through a rough time in your life, and we should all be kind enough to show a little mercy when we can." Courtney truly felt terrible for ever thinking poorly of Linda.

"You're very kind. The thing is, you won't have to deal with me much longer. I've found a little part time job at one of the department stores over in the Ruby Cove mall. I was spending a lot of time there, anyway, and one of the cashiers told me I ought to apply for their opening. I do like being here, and I'd still like to volunteer occasionally, but I think it would be much safer if I'm just putting a dress on the wrong rack instead of a dog in the wrong cage."

They both laughed a bit over that one, and Courtney smiled warmly at her. "You'll have a wonderful time there, Linda. You just give me a call when you need to come snuggle a dog or a cat, and we'll make sure it happens."

"I also want to apologize to you for something else." Linda twisted her hands in front of her.

Courtney's eyebrows crept toward each other in concern. "What's that?"

"Well, you've been polite enough not to mention it, but I'm sure you know that I was taken into police custody under suspicion of murder. Of course, I didn't do it, but I'm sure the whole town knew about it considering how much gossip floats around Curly Bay."

That was true enough. Courtney was just thrilled to know that it wasn't Linda after all, and she was glad she hadn't confronted her about it. "If you didn't do it, then why should you apologize?"

"Because it probably looked bad on the shelter," Linda explained.

"I wouldn't worry about that," Courtney assured her. "Mrs. McKenzie was doing her best to make this place look bad without anyone's help. What happened, though?" She knew Detective Fletcher would probably give her all the details later, anyway, but it didn't hurt to have them from Linda.

"I was really shocked when the police showed up and wanted to take me in for questioning," Linda explained with a sigh. "I knew I was innocent, so of course I obliged. I had no idea who Tyler Lancaster was. I'd never heard of him or met him. It turned out he was my twin sister's husband. You'll remember I told you that I'd distanced myself from my family quite some time ago, and we truly didn't have any contact with each other. I always knew there would be trouble with them, but I never realized it would be this bad.

"Anyway," she continued. "The last I knew, my sister Ann had been married to a Ted Sherman. I guess she got divorced and then married Tyler. It turns out that Tyler had a big gambling problem, and it was getting so bad that they couldn't pay their bills. Collectors were showing up at their doorstep and constantly calling her, and they were about to lose their home. Ann tried to talk to Tyler, but he'd just tell her he was handling it and that everything would be fine. My sister knew it *wouldn't* be fine, and she'd already fought so hard to get herself back on her feet after her divorce. She got upset, and she was tired of Tyler not listening to her. She took the drastic way out, figuring she could get his life insurance and pay all the bills." Linda shook her head. "It's just tragic."

"How do you know all this?" Courtney asked. "You said you hadn't spoken to your sister in years."

Linda gave a sad smile. "She called me when she was arrested. We talked for a long time. It was actually kind of nice, despite the circumstances. I know she's going to jail, but I think we'll start talking again. It's nice to have my sister back."

"Good for you." Courtney patted her hand just as the bell over the front door sounded. "I'd better go see what that's about."

She was astonished to see that Mrs. McKenzie had come back. She no longer looked angry, fortunately. "Courtney, I'm so sorry to come back and bother you once again. I know you have no reason to extend me even the slightest bit of courtesy after all I've put you through. I've been absolutely terrible, but I was wondering if..." She trailed off as she twisted her hands through Angus's leash and tears glistened in her eyes.

Courtney had never seen Mrs. McKenzie quite like this before. "What is it? I'm happy to help," she said softly.

"Well, I'm so glad to have my Angus back. I love him to little bitty pieces, and I'm so glad he's the same, stuffy little guy I know him to be. But I think I also fell in love with Bruce while I had him. He's so sweet, and the poor boy must want a home. I can't imagine how he must feel to be put back in a cage after living for a week in a home, and snuggling with me in bed, and going for walks. Like I said, I know you don't have any reason to say yes, but I was wondering if I could adopt him."

"You're right," Courtney said, frowning. "You have put me through a lot. It's been difficult, and for a minute there I thought you really were trying to ruin this place and all that we've worked so hard for."

Mrs. McKenzie's shoulders sagged in disappointment.

"But," Courtney continued, "I know that you were pushing that hard because you genuinely thought something had happened to Angus. You wanted him to be okay, and you weren't going to stop until you had the answers. If we'd been negligent in some way, you didn't want anyone else to suffer the same way you were. I have to admire that kind of devotion in someone."

"Really?" Mrs. McKenzie practically squealed.

"Let's see what Bruce thinks of this."

Linda was already on it, and she brought the little terrier out from his kennel and set him on the floor. Bruce happily trotted over to Mrs. McKenzie, panting and wagging his tail. Angus sniffed him thoroughly and gave just the slightest wag of his tail, which was more emotion than he normally showed.

Linda looked up at Courtney and smiled. "What do you think? Another set of happy twins?"

Courtney grinned. "Yeah, I think so. I'll get the paperwork started."

THANK YOU FOR CHOOSING A PUREREAD BOOK!

We hope you enjoyed the story, and as a way to thank you for choosing PureRead we'd like to send you this free Special Edition Cozy, and other fun reader rewards...

Click Here to download your free Cozy Mystery
PureRead.com/cozy

Thanks again for reading.

See you soon!

OTHER BOOKS IN THIS SERIES

The Missing Pom Mystery

The Case of the Confused Canine

A Case Full of Cats

A Furry case of Foul Play

The Case of a Beagle and a Body

A Case of Canines, Cats, & Costumes

A Case of Frauds and Friendly Lizards

A Very Furry Christmas Mystery

The Mysterious Case of Books, Barks, & Burglary

A Shocking Case of Party Animals

A Strange Case of Pretty Puppies and Petty Theft

The Troubling Case of Summer Punches & Picnic
Puppies

A Feisty Case Of Festive Murder

A Catty Case of Mayor's Murder

Also, be sure to join our Reader Club (100% free)

PureRead.com/cozy

OUR GIFT TO YOU

AS A WAY TO SAY THANK YOU WE WOULD
LOVE TO SEND YOU THIS SPECIAL EDITION
COZY MYSTERY FREE OF CHARGE.

Our Reader List is 100% FREE

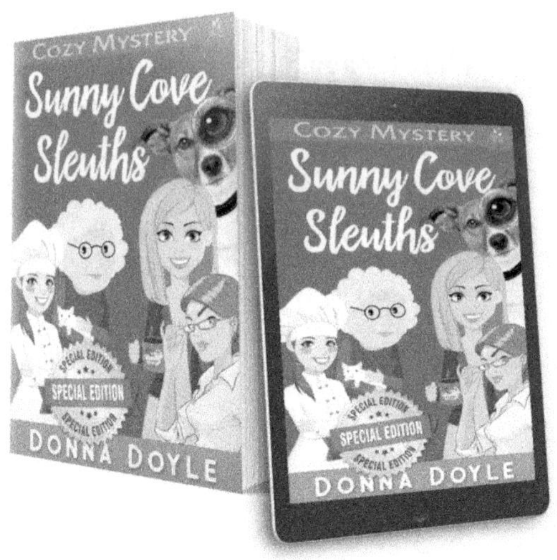

Click Here to download your free Cozy Mystery

PureRead.com/cozy

At PureRead we publish books you can trust. Great tales without smut or swearing, but with all of the mystery and romance you expect from a great story.

Be the first to know when we release new books, take part in our fun competitions, and get surprise free books in your inbox by signing up to our Reader list.

As a thank you you'll receive this exclusive Special Edition Cozy available only to our subscribers...

Click Here to download your free Cozy Mystery
PureRead.com/cozy

Thanks again for reading.
See you soon!

www.ingramcontent.com/pod-product-compliance
Lightning Source LLC
Chambersburg PA
CBHW051432150726
48000CB00005B/2067